Carolyn King

OXFORD

Chapter 1

Dishes, Dishes

Dishes, dishes everywhere, but not a bite to eat.

Flora the Maid had to do all the washing-up, but she never sat down to eat. Mrs Stint was too lazy to do the work herself. Her daughter Grizel was too spoiled. So Flora had to cook all the meals and serve them.

Flora had to clear all the dishes and wash them. Mrs Stint did not even pay her. She did not even say thank you! No, Mrs Stint had a heart as hard as flint.

Mrs Stint and Grizel hated Flora. They hated her because her heart was warm and kind.

Mrs Stint and Grizel loved only money. And money is a cold, hard thing to keep in your heart.

One day they said to Flora, "All these years you have lived in our house, and you never paid us a penny for rent."

"I never had a penny," said Flora (which was true).

"Well, go out and earn some! Don't come back until you can pay one golden pound!"

So away went poor Flora, though she had nowhere to go, no one to look after her and no one to hold her hand.

Chapter 2

"Who Will Pity a Pot?"

She walked until she came to an old, broken-down shack. There, outside, stood one old bucket and one dirty iron cauldron, red with rust.

No. Close up, it was not rust-red. The pot was red hot. And out of it came a voice like crackling twigs.

Who will pity a pot?

I am hotter than hot!

I have no daughter

To pour on cool water.

Oh, who will help? Who?

Is it you? Is it you?

"Me?" said Flora. Stepping closer, she peeped inside the cauldron.

There was nothing inside but dirt, years and years of dirt. It was the pot itself that was speaking.

"Water! Water!" it whispered.

At once, Flora picked up the bucket and ran down to the river.

The water at the edge was muddy, so she waded out deep. Then she scooped up water from the clear, cool, middle of the stream.

Flora hurried back and threw the water –

HISSSS!

– over the red-hot pot.

The cauldron gave a sigh of delight and danced on its three legs.

Because she was a kind girl, Flora began to scrub the pot clean. While she worked, night came down.

In the darkness the cauldron chattered.

"I am the cauldron of the Waltzing Warlock. His magic is so foul that it stains me like tar."

Flora looked around her.

"Surely he does not live in that tumbledown shed?"

"Things are not always what they seem," said the cauldron. "*Inside,* the house is lovely. But don't go in unless you can talk your way out again … Keep safe! Go home."

"Oh, but I can't go home until I have earned a pound!" Flora explained. "I must repay Mrs Stint!"

"Well then, I shall tell you how to get a whole bucket of gold. But listen carefully and do just as I say. Or in the morning *you* will not be holding *me* – *I* shall be holding *you*. My master will cook you for his breakfast!"

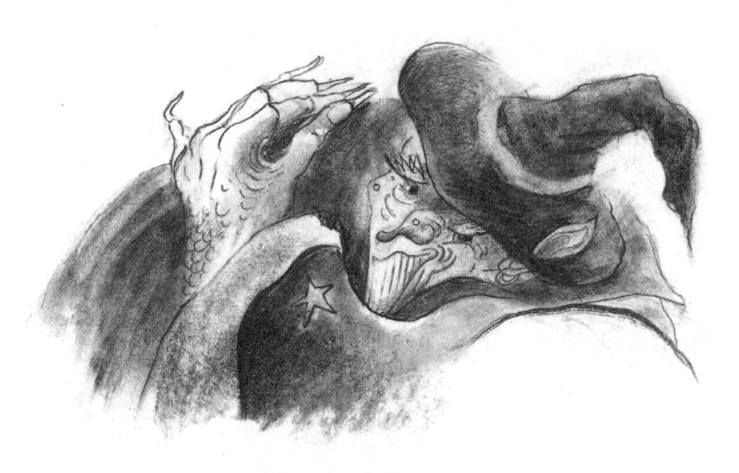

Chapter 3

The Waltzing Warlock

Flora went over to the tumbledown hut. She pushed with her shoulder at the sagging door.

Cobwebs stretched. The hinges groaned. Surely this door had not been open for a hundred years!

But in went brave little Flora, clutching her courage like a bunch of flowers.

The pot had spoken true. The inside of the shack was very different from the outside. It was thirteen times bigger, with thirteen rooms and thirteen doors.

Each room was more beautiful than the last. The walls were lined with gold glass mirrors, and the ceilings hung with lamps.

There was a chandelier made from a million tears.

An invisible orchestra started playing on golden fiddles.

The music was so shrill that dogs began howling all over the world.

Flora gazed around her in delighted amazement. She had never been inside a palace before.

In the thirteenth room sat the Waltzing Warlock himself. He was writing spells, in poison, with the tip of his scorpion tail. At the sight of Flora, he jumped up.

"Come in! Come in, my dear! I have been waiting for you. The dancing cannot begin until I have a partner.

"I have been hoping for someone just like you. Give me your hand and let us dance!"

Flora curtseyed. "Thank you kindly, Sir. For a bucket of gold I will gladly dance with you."

At once the bucket in her hand was so full of gold that Flora had to set it down.

"Now let the dancing begin!" cried the Waltzing Warlock.

But Flora looked down at her ragged clothes.

"Oh, Sir, my dress! I cannot dance in such a shabby old thing."

The magician went to his books to look up a spell. There was a flash of magic fire. And using the flames, he stitched a gown of fiery taffeta.

"Oh!" cried Flora. "I never had a new dress before! Mrs Stint would not even buy me an apron. I never dreamed of wearing a Paris gown!"

The taffeta skirts swished deliciously. Very, very slowly, Flora put the dress on.

"Time is wasting!" the Warlock cried. "Do let us dance!"

But Flora looked down at her feet. "Oh, Sir, how can I dance my best wearing these worn-out shoes?"

The Warlock frowned. He looked up a shoe-spell and … *flash!* In a splash of silver, there stood a pair of scarlet shoes.

Flora admired them for a long time. Then slowly, slowly, she slipped her feet inside.

"Now do let us dance!" cried the Waltzing Warlock, showing his teeth in a purple grin.

"Oh, but it is so hot, Sir! I might faint ... without a fan to cool me!"

After the fan, she asked for gloves.
After the gloves, she asked for a cloak.
After the cloak, she asked for a ribbon.
After the ribbon, she asked for a comb.

Then Flora spent a long, long time combing her pretty hair.

The Warlock grew angry and impatient. He ground his teeth and clenched his fists. But every time Flora asked for something, he had to fetch it.

His magic would not work until she danced with him.

Now, don't go thinking that Flora was greedy. She had never asked for anything before – no, not in all her life. It seemed very rude to ask now.

But the Old Iron Pot had told her what to do, because she had been kind and because it liked her.

After the comb, she asked for a bracelet. After the bracelet, she asked for silk stockings. After the stockings, she asked for a drink of melted snow from the mountains of Nepal.

She asked for Turkish delight from Turkey and roses from Persia. She asked for perfume from Arabia and an ostrich egg from Africa (lightly boiled).

It was difficult for a girl like Flora to keep on asking. She had never been given a present before – no, not in all her life.

But on and on she asked, because the Old Iron Pot had told her to.

She asked for a banquet from Bali. She asked for a glass coach from the Land of Fairy Tales.

Black night was turning grey. Soon day would dawn.

Flora was weary; she could think of nothing else to ask for.

Fearfully, she joined hands with the Waltzing Warlock. His skin was lizard-cold and scratchy.

Slowly, they began to dance.

Chapter 4

Flora Comes Home

"Cock-a-doodle-doo!" The first cock crowed.

The Waltzing Warlock swore horribly. He stamped his foot ... then disappeared! Flora's arms were empty! It was as if he had melted in the first ray of sunlight.

Flora drove home in her glass coach. She looked like a queen as she waved to people in the street.

The bucket of gold sat on the red velvet seat next to her.

Flora took one gold coin from the bucket and gave it to Mrs Stint.

"All these years, you have fed me on crusts of bread. All these years, you have dressed me in rags. I have added up all your kindnesses to me, and here is the money I owe you. Keep the change."

Mrs Stint stared. So did her daughter.

"How did you do it?" demanded Grizel.

So Flora explained. She told the tale of the Old Iron Pot. She described the tumbledown shed and the magician inside it. She explained about asking him for all those presents.

Chapter 5

Greedy Grizel

Away went Grizel, taking the glass coach without even asking.

She drove until she found the shack. There was the cauldron standing at the roadside, calling:

Who will pity a pot?

I am hotter than hot!

And I have no daughter

To pour on cool water.

Oh, who will help? Who?

Is it you? Is it you?

Grizel was in a hurry to get her presents. So she only scooped up half a bucket of muddy water to throw over the cauldron.

"You have covered me in mud!" groaned the Old Iron Pot. "Won't you scrub me clean?"

"What do you think I am? A servant like Flora?" said Grizel.

Into the shack went Grizel. She did not stop to admire the gold-glass mirrors. She did not notice ceilings hung with lamps. She did not even glance up at the chandelier made of a million tears.

"Soon I shall have a better palace than this!" she thought.

She did not even stop to listen to the orchestra of golden fiddles. No, she ran straight through twelve rooms until she reached the thirteenth.

There sat the Waltzing Warlock, scratching spells with one fingernail. Seeing Grizel, he jumped up.

"Come in! Come in, my dear! I have been waiting for you. The dancing cannot begin until I have a partner!

"I have been hoping for someone just like you. Give me your hand and let us dance!"

"Not till you give me a dress, a coach, a ribbon, a comb, a feast, a cloak, a fan, a bracelet and this bucket full of gold."

Grizel marked them off on her fingers. She remembered every single present Flora had won.

"A muff, some shoes and a drink ..."

With one, single, smelly spell, the Warlock granted all her greedy wishes.

"Anything else?" he asked. His dark eyes flickered with joy.

Grizel racked her brains, but she could not think of anything. She had asked for it all, and the whole night lay ahead.

So she joined hands with the Waltzing Warlock. The golden fiddles shrilled. The room spun. And Grizel whirled in the Warlock's arms.

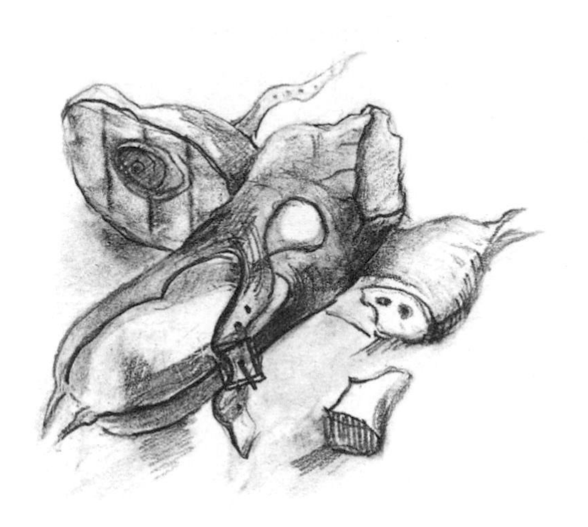

Chapter 6

"I'd Really Rather Not"

Faster and faster they danced, till her new shoes wore through. The hems of her dress frayed into rags.

Faster and faster they whirled, till her combed hair tangled and her ribbons came untied.

Faster and faster went the dance. They whirled so fast that Grizel was soon too dizzy to speak. She danced and danced until she was as hot as the Warlock's old iron pot.

At last, the Waltzing Warlock slowed and stopped. Grizel fell down to the ground, and lay there, limply. She had no breath left for speaking.

The Waltzing Warlock carried Grizel outside, meaning to cook her for his breakfast.

But when he put her into the Old Iron Pot, the pot was not hot. In fact it was as cold as a ship's bell at the bottom of the sea.

The Warlock cried:

"*Come Pot! Heat!*
It's time to eat!"

The cauldron shuffled its three iron feet.

"I'd really rather not," said the Old Iron Pot.

The Waltzing Warlock ground his purple teeth. His cauldron had never argued with him before. The Warlock was tired and hungry after so much dancing. The brightness of the moon hurt his purple eyes.

"Cook my breakfast, I say!
Or shall I fetch my book of spells
and turn you into a coal bucket?"

The Old Iron Pot trembled so hard that it rang like a church bell. But it stayed as cold as winter.

The Waltzing Warlock twirled his knotty eyebrows and stamped his foot. "I shall heat you so hot that you melt on the spot!" he hissed.

Then he went back into the shack to fetch his magic book. He slammed the door so hard that the shack trembled, too.

In the bottom of The Old Iron Pot lay Grizel, like a handful of chicken bones. Surely, nothing could save her now!

Except, perhaps, Flora.

Chapter 7

The Cauldron's Revenge

Because she was a kind girl, Flora had followed the glass coach on foot. She was afraid for Grizel.

Now she came dancing along the moonlit road, like a lick of flame in her red taffeta dress. Her red satin shoes kicked up the dust.

As soon as she saw the Old Iron Pot plastered in mud, she guessed what had happened.

As soon as she saw Grizel lying in the pot, all torn and tired and tearful, she guessed what had happened.

As soon as she felt the cold sides of the Old Iron Pot, she guessed what had happened.

Flora crouched down beside the cauldron and gave it a kiss.

Then she began to polish it clean with her red taffeta dress. And as she worked, she whispered.

The Warlock came out of his tumbledown shack and looked to the right and the left. There was no one to be seen on the moonlit road.

"I will give you one last chance," he told the cauldron.

"I want to eat,
So heat, Pot, heat!"

The Old Iron Pot shuffled its iron feet.

"*Dance with me, master,*
faster and faster.
Then I'll grow hot,"
said the Old Iron Pot.

"Dance with *you?*" snorted the Warlock. "I have a good mind to tie your three legs together and throw you in the river!

"Dance with you, indeed! You have three legs and all of them are left-footed!"

"All the better to waltz with you, master," said the saucy pot.

But as the Warlock went to kick the pot, he saw something. He saw *himself*. In the shiny sides of the cauldron, he saw his own reflection. His reflection looked back at him.

Then it poked out its tongue!

In a rage, the Warlock grasped hold of the cauldron by its two big handles, and began to lug it down to the river.

But the pot began to dance.

One-two-three, one-two-three, went its three iron feet. It waltzed quite well. *One-two-three, one-two-three.* The pot spun the Warlock round and round.

Faster and faster they danced. In at the door of the shack and through all the thirteen rooms.

They danced all the pile off the carpets and shook all the cuckoos out of the clocks.

The shrill fiddles played higher and higher, until their strings broke. Music still streamed from the tips of the Warlock's hair. He pressed his cheek to the cauldron.

They danced till the roof caught light and the mirrors melted.

They danced till the tears of the chandeliers were all dried.

They danced till the moon set and the bats went back to bed.

They danced till the magician's robe was in tatters and his hooves wore thin.

They danced till the Warlock himself was thinner than thread.

The shack was shaken to pieces, but the cauldron danced on and on.

Chapter 8

Flora's Travels

When at last the cauldron waltzed to a halt, the sun was up and there was nothing left of the Whirling Warlock. Only his scorpion sting lay on the sunlit road, as big as a baby's rattle.

A face peeped out over the rim of the cauldron. It was grim and grimy and green.

"I want to go home now," said Grizel. "I don't feel very well."

Not Flora. Flora never went home.

Lazy Grizel and Mrs Stint had to do their own housework and cook their own meals. What a terrible job they made of it!

Flora cooked, too.

She travelled the world in the glass coach, with a shiny iron pot on the roof. She travelled the whole wide world and farther, cooking at harvest suppers and weddings.

She cooked for circus crowds and ships full of sailors. She cooked on May Day and Midsummer's Eve.

She cooked rice pudding in the Old Iron Pot. And anyone who tasted that pudding said it was the best ever made. I know that's true, because I ate some …

But I don't remember who did the washing-up.

About the author

I love a good folk tale – the scarier the better. So that is why I chose to retell this one about a wizard with an appetite for life – preferably the life of someone rather greedy and very light on her feet!

In the original story there is no happy ending for Grizel. But that is the marvellous thing about being an author: you can make any story turn out just the way you want.

How would you have made it end, I wonder?